Blacky the Crow

DOVER
CHILDREN'S THRIFT CLASSICS

Blacky the Crow

THORNTON W. BURGESS

Illustrated by Harrison Cady

PUBLISHED IN ASSOCIATION WITH THE
THORNTON W. BURGESS MUSEUM AND THE
GREEN BRIAR NATURE CENTER, SANDWICH, MASSACHUSETTS
by
DOVER PUBLICATIONS, INC.
Mineola, New York

DOVER CHILDREN'S THRIFT CLASSICS
EDITOR OF THIS VOLUME: PAUL NEGRI

Copyright

Copyright © 1999 by Dover Publications, Inc.
All rights reserved under Pan American and International Copyright Conventions.

Bibliographical Note

This Dover edition, first published in 1999 in association with the Thornton W. Burgess Museum and the Green Briar Nature Center, Sandwich, Massachusetts, who have provided a new introduction, is an unabridged republication of the edition published by Grosset & Dunlap in 1922.

Library of Congress Cataloging-in-Publication Data

Burgess, Thornton W. (Thornton Waldo), 1874–1965.
   Blacky the crow / Thornton W. Burgess ; illustrations by Harrison Cady.
      p.   cm. — (Dover children's thrift classics)
   Summary: Blacky the clever crow shares adventures with other animals in the Green Meadows and by the Big River, as he considers stealing eggs from Hooty the owl, helps Farmer Brown's boy protect Dusty the wood duck, and engages in other escapades.
   ISBN 0-486-40550-8 (pbk.)
   [1. Crows—Fiction. 2. Animals—Fiction.] I. Cady, Harrison, 1877–
ill. II. Title. III. Series.
PZ7.B917Bg   1999
[Fic]—dc21   99-10879
                                                  CIP

Manufactured in the United States of America
Dover Publications, Inc., 31 East 2nd Street, Mineola, N.Y. 11501

Dedication

To an American citizen who, despite persecution and changed conditions, has by his adaptability and intelligence maintained his place in the land of his forefathers—the crow

Introduction to the Dover Edition

The Adventures of Blacky the Crow is just one out of 170 different books that Thornton W. Burgess wrote for children. Mr. Burgess grew up in the small Cape Cod town of Sandwich, Massachusetts. As a boy, he became familiar with the backroads and woodlands as he did errands to help support his family. He encountered many animals in his daily treks through the woods. After he left Sandwich, Mr. Burgess never forgot these special places. He went on to write about them in different nature stories for children. These tales are just as entertaining today as they were when they were written over 80 years ago. If you come to Sandwich, you can visit the Dear Old Briar Patch and the Smiling Pool at the Green Briar Nature Center. The Thornton W. Burgess Society is a non-profit environmental education organization that carries on the work of Mr. Burgess through programs and exhibits about nature. The Society operates the Green Briar Nature Center and the Thornton W. Burgess Museum. You can learn more about Thornton W. Burgess and the Society through our webpage at http://www.capecod.net/tburgess

The Adventures of Blacky the Crow was first published in 1922. Blacky the Crow is one of Thornton W. Burgess's smartest characters. But alas, Blacky's sharp eyes often get him in trouble like his cousin Sammy Jay. He enjoys playing tricks on the other animals of the Green Forest and Green Meadows. In this story, learn how Blacky tries hard to outwit Hooty and Mrs. Hooty the Owl to get some of their eggs. First, Blacky must decide how hungry he is and how badly he wants those eggs to even consider crossing Hooty the Owl or Mrs. Hooty. Hooty has a very sharp bill and big claws and Mrs. Hooty is even fiercer! In another chapter, read how Blacky does a good deed by working with Farmer Brown's boy to protect Dusty the Wood Duck and his friends from hunters. We hope that you enjoy reading about Blacky and all his friends in the Green Meadows and Big River.

Contents

x   Contents

List of Illustrations

I. Blacky the Crow Makes a Discovery

BLACKY THE Crow is always watching for things not intended for his sharp eyes. The result is that he gets into no end of trouble which he could avoid. In this respect he is just like his cousin, Sammy Jay. Between them they see a great deal with which they have no business and which it would be better for them not to see.

Now Blacky the Crow finds it no easy matter to pick up a living when snow covers the Green Meadows and the Green Forest, and ice binds the Big River and the Smiling Pool. He has to use his sharp eyes for all they are worth in order to find enough to fill his stomach, and he will eat anything in the way of food that he can swallow. Often he travels long distances looking for food, but at night he always comes back to the same place in the Green Forest, to sleep in company with others of his family.

Blacky dearly loves company, particularly at night, and about the time jolly, round, red Mr. Sun is beginning to think about his bed behind the Purple Hills, you will find Blacky heading for a certain part of the Green Forest where he knows he will have neighbors of his own kind. Peter Rabbit says that it is because Blacky's conscience troubles him so that he doesn't dare sleep alone, but Happy Jack Squirrel says that Blacky hasn't any conscience. You can believe just which you please, though I suspect that neither of them really knows.

As I have said, Blacky is quite a traveler at this time of year, and sometimes his search for food takes him to out-of-the-way places. One day toward the very last of winter, the notion entered his black head that he would have a look in a certain lonesome corner of the Green Forest

where once upon a time Redtail the Hawk had lived.
Blacky knew well enough that Redtail wasn't there now;
he had gone south in the fall and wouldn't be back until
he was sure that Mistress Spring had arrived on the Green
Meadows and in the Green Forest.

Like the black imp he is, Blacky flew over the tree-tops,
his sharp eyes watching for something interesting below.
Presently he saw ahead of him the old nest of Redtail. He
knew all about that nest. He had visited it before when
Redtail was away. Still it might be worth another visit. You
never can tell what you may find in old houses. Now, of
course, Blacky knew perfectly well that Redtail was miles
and miles, hundreds of miles away, and so there was nothing to fear from him. But Blacky learned ever so long ago
that there is nothing like making sure that there is no danger. So, instead of flying straight to that old nest, he first
flew over the tree so that he could look down into it.

Right away he saw something that made him gasp and
blink his eyes. It was quite large and white, and it
looked—it looked very much indeed like an egg! Do you
wonder that Blacky gasped and blinked? Here was snow
on the ground, and Rough Brother North Wind and Jack
Frost had given no hint that they were even thinking of
going back to the Far North. The idea of any one laying an
egg at this time of year! Blacky flew over to a tall pine-tree
to think it over.

"Must be it was a little lump of snow," thought he. "Yet
if ever I saw an egg, that looked like one. Jumping
grasshoppers, how good an egg would taste right now!"
You know Blacky has a weakness for eggs. The more he
thought about it, the hungrier he grew. Several times he
almost made up his mind to fly straight over there and
make sure, but he didn't quite dare. If it were an egg, it
must belong to somebody, and perhaps it would be best
to find out who. Suddenly Blacky shook himself. "I must
be dreaming," said he. "There couldn't, there just couldn't
be an egg at this time of year, or in that old tumble-down
nest! I'll just fly away and forget it."

So he flew away, but he couldn't forget it. He kept thinking of it all day, and when he went to sleep that night he made up his mind to have another look at that old nest.

II. Blacky Makes Sure

"As true as ever I've cawed a caw
That was a new-laid egg I saw."

"WHAT ARE YOU talking about?" demanded Sammy
Jay, coming up just in time to hear the last part of
what Blacky the Crow was mumbling to himself.

"Oh nothing, Cousin, nothing at all," replied Blacky. "I
was just talking foolishness to myself."

Sammy looked at him sharply. "You aren't feeling sick,
are you, Cousin Blacky?" he asked. "Must be something
the matter with you when you begin talking about new-
laid eggs, when everything's covered with snow and ice.
Foolishness is no name for it. Whoever heard of such a
thing as a new-laid egg this time of year?"

"Nobody, I guess," replied Blacky. "I told you I was just
talking foolishness. You see, I'm so hungry that I just got
to thinking what I'd have if I could have anything I wanted.
That made me think of eggs, and I tried to think just how
I would feel if I should suddenly see a great big egg right
in front of me. I guess I must have said something about
it."

"I guess you must have. It isn't egg time yet, and it won't
be for a long time. Take my advice and just forget about
impossible things. I'm going over to Farmer Brown's corn-
crib. Corn may not be as good as eggs, but it is very good
and very filling. Better come along," said Sammy.

"Not this morning, thank you. Some other time, perhaps," replied Blacky.

He watched Sammy disappear through the trees. Then
he flew to the top of the tallest pine-tree to make sure that

4

no one was about. When he was quite sure that no one was watching him, he spread his wings and headed for the most lonesome corner of the Green Forest.

"I'm foolish. I know I'm foolish," he muttered. "But I've just got to have another look in that old nest of Redtail the Hawk. I just can't get it out of my head that that was an egg, a great, big, white egg, that I saw there yesterday. It won't do any harm to have another look, anyway."

Straight toward the tree in which was the great tumble-down nest of Redtail the Hawk he flew, and as he drew near, he flew high, for Blacky is too shrewd and smart to take any chances. Not that he thought that there could be any danger there; but you never can tell, and it is always the part of wisdom to be on the safe side. As he passed over the top of the tree, he looked down eagerly. Just imagine how he felt when instead of one, he saw *two* white things in the old nest,—two white things that looked for all the world like eggs! The day before there had been but one; now there were *two*. That settled it in Blacky's mind; they were eggs! They couldn't be anything else.

Blacky kept right on flying. Somehow he didn't dare stop just then. He was too much excited by what he had discovered to think clearly. He had got to have time to get his wits together. Whoever had laid those eggs was big and strong. He felt sure of that. It must be some one a great deal bigger than himself, and he was of no mind to get into trouble, even for a dinner of fresh eggs. He must first find out whose they were; then he would know better what to do. He felt sure that no one else knew about them, and he knew that they couldn't run away. So he kept right on flying until he reached a certain tall pine-tree where he could sit and think without being disturbed.

"Eggs!" he muttered. "Real eggs! Now who under the sun can have moved into Redtail's old house? And what can they mean by laying eggs before Mistress Spring has even sent word that she has started? It's too much for me. It certainly is too much for me."

III. Blacky Finds Out Who Owns the Eggs

TWO BIG white eggs in a tumble-down nest, and snow and ice everywhere! Did ever anybody hear of such a thing before?

"Wouldn't believe it, if I hadn't seen it with my own eyes," muttered Blacky the Crow. "Have to believe them. If I can't believe them, it's of no use to try to believe anything in this world. As sure as I sit here, that old nest has two eggs in it. Whoever laid them must be crazy to start housekeeping at this time of year. I must find out whose eggs they are and then—"

Blacky didn't finish, but there was a hungry look in his eyes that would have told any who saw it, had there been any to see it, that he had a use for those eggs. But there was none to see it, and he took the greatest care that there should be none to see him when he once again started for a certain lonesome corner of the Green Forest.

"First I'll make sure that the eggs are still there," thought he, and flew high above the tree tops, so that as he passed over the tree in which was the old nest of Red-tail the Hawk, he might look down into it. To have seen him, you would never have guessed that he was looking for anything in particular. He seemed to be just flying over on his way to some distant place. If the eggs were still there, he meant to come back and hide in the top of a near-by pine-tree to watch until he was sure that he might safely steal those eggs, or to find out whose they were.

Blacky's heart beat fast with excitement as he drew near that old tumble-down nest. Would those two big white eggs be there? Perhaps there would be three! The very thought made him flap his wings a little faster. A few

6

more wing strokes and he would be right over the tree. How he did hope to see those eggs! He could almost see into the nest now. One stroke! Two strokes! Three strokes! Blacky bit his tongue to keep from giving a sharp caw of disappointment and surprise.

There were no eggs to be seen. No, Sir, there wasn't a sign of eggs in that old nest. There wasn't because—why, do you think? There wasn't because Blacky looked straight down on a great mass of feathers which quite covered them from sight, and he didn't have to look twice to know that that great mass of feathers was really a great bird, the bird to whom those eggs belonged.

Blacky didn't turn to come back as he had planned. He kept right on, just as if he hadn't seen anything, and as he flew he shivered a little. He shivered at the thought of what might have happened to him if he had tried to steal those eggs the day before and had been caught doing it.

"I'm thankful I knew enough to leave them alone," said he. "Funny I never once guessed whose eggs they are. I might have known that no one but Hooty the Horned Owl would think of nesting at this time of year. And that was Mrs. Hooty I saw on the nest just now. My, but she's big! She's bigger than Hooty himself! Yes, Sir, it's a lucky thing I didn't try to get those eggs yesterday. Probably both Hooty and Mrs. Hooty were sitting close by, only they were sitting so still that I thought they were parts of the tree they were in. Blacky, Blacky, the sooner you forget those eggs the better."

> "Some things are best forgotten
> As soon as they are learned.
> Who never plays with fire
> Will surely not get burned."

IV. The Cunning of Blacky

NOW WHEN Blacky the Crow discovered that the eggs in the old tumble-down nest of Redtail the Hawk in a lonesome corner of the Green Forest belonged to Hooty the Owl, he straightway made the best of resolutions; he would simply forget all about those eggs. He would forget that he ever had seen them, and he would stay away from that corner of the Green Forest. That was a very wise resolution. Of all the people who live in the Green Forest, none is fiercer or more savage than Hooty the Owl, unless it is Mrs. Hooty. She is bigger than Hooty and certainly quite as much to be feared by the little people.

All this Blacky knows. No one knows it better. And Blacky is not one to poke his head into trouble with his eyes open. So he very wisely resolved to forget all about those eggs. Now it is one thing to make a resolution and quite another thing to live up to it, as you all know. It was easy enough to say that he would forget, but not at all easy to forget. It would have been different if it had been spring or early summer, when there were plenty of other eggs to be had by any one smart enough to find them and steal them. But now, when it was still winter (such an unheard-of time for any one to have eggs!), and it was hard work to find enough to keep a hungry Crow's stomach filled, the thought of those eggs *would* keep popping into his head. He just *couldn't* seem to forget them. After a little, he didn't try.

Now Blacky the Crow is very, very cunning. He is one of the smartest of all the little people who fly. No one can get into more mischief and still keep out of trouble than can Blacky the Crow. That is because he uses the wits in that black head of his. In fact, some people are unkind enough to say that he spends all his spare time in planning mischief. The more he thought of those eggs, the more he wanted them, and it wasn't long before he began to try to plan some way to get them without risking his own precious skin.

"I can't do it alone," thought he, "and yet if I take any one into my secret, I'll have to share those eggs. That won't do at all, because I want them myself. I found them, and I ought to have them." He quite forgot or overlooked the fact that those eggs really belonged to Hooty and Mrs. Hooty and to no one else. "Now let me see, what can I do?"

He thought and he thought and he thought and he thought, and little by little a plan worked out in his little black head. Then he chuckled. He chuckled right out loud, then hurriedly looked around to see if any one had heard him. No one had, so he chuckled again. He cocked his head on one side and half closed his eyes, as if that plan was something he could see and he was looking at it very hard. Then he cocked his head on the other side and did the same thing.

"It's all right," said he at last. "It'll give my relatives a lot of fun, and of course they will be very grateful to me for that. It won't hurt Hooty or Mrs. Hooty a bit, but it will make them very angry. They have very short tempers, and people with short tempers usually forget everything else when they are angry. We'll pay them a visit while the sun is bright, because then perhaps they cannot see well enough to catch us, and we'll tease them until they lose their tempers and forget all about keeping guard over those eggs. Then I'll slip in and get one and perhaps both of them. Without knowing that they are doing anything of the kind, my friends and relatives will help me to get a good meal. My, how good those eggs will taste!"

It was a very clever and cunning plan, for Blacky is a very clever and cunning rascal, but of course it didn't deserve success because nothing that means needless worry and trouble for others deserves to succeed.

V. Blacky Calls His Friends

When Blacky cries "Caw, caw, caw, caw!"
As if he'd dislocate his jaw,
His relatives all hasten where
He waits them with a crafty air.

THEY KNOW that there is mischief afoot, and the Crow
family is always ready for mischief. So on this particular morning when they heard Blacky cawing at the top of
his lungs from the tallest pine-tree in the Green Forest,
they hastened over there as fast as they could fly, calling
to each other excitedly and sure that they were going to
have a good time of some kind.

Blacky chuckled as he saw them coming. "Come on!
Come on! Caw, caw, caw! Hurry up and flap your wings
faster. I know where Hooty the Owl is, and we'll have no
end of fun with him," he cried.

"Caw, caw, caw, caw, caw, caw!" shouted all his relatives
in great glee. "Where is he? Lead us to him. We'll drive him
out of the Green Forest!"

So Blacky led the way over to the most lonesome corner of the Green Forest, straight to the tree in which
Hooty the Owl was comfortably sleeping. Blacky had
taken pains to slip over early that morning and make sure
just where he was. He had discovered Hooty fast asleep,
and he knew that he would remain right where he was
until dark. You know Hooty's eyes are not meant for much
use in bright light, and the brighter the light, the more uncomfortable his eyes feel. Blacky knows this, too, and he
had chosen the very brightest part of the morning to call
his relatives over to torment poor Hooty. Jolly, round,

10

bright Mr. Sun was shining his very brightest, and the white snow on the ground made it seem brighter still. Even Blacky had to blink, and he knew that poor Hooty would find it harder still.

But one thing Blacky was very careful not to even hint of, and that was that Mrs. Hooty was right close at hand. Mrs. Hooty is bigger and even more fierce than Hooty, and Blacky didn't want to frighten any of the more timid of his relatives. What he hoped down deep in his crafty heart was that when they got to teasing and tormenting Hooty and making the great racket which he knew they would, Mrs. Hooty would lose her temper and fly over to join Hooty in trying to drive away the black tormentors. Then Blacky would slip over to the nest which she had left unguarded and steal one and perhaps both of the eggs he knew were there.

When they reached the tree where Hooty was, he was blinking his great yellow eyes and had fluffed out all his feathers, which is a way he has when he is angry, to make himself look twice as big as he really is. Of course, he had heard the noisy crew coming, and he knew well enough what to expect. As soon as they saw him, they began to scream as loud as ever they could and to call him all manner of names. The boldest of them would dart at him as if to pull out a mouthful of feathers, but took the greatest care not to get too near. You see, the way Hooty hissed and snapped his great bill was very threatening, and they knew that if once he got hold of one of them with those big cruel claws of his, that would be the end.

So they were content to simply scold and scream at him and fly around him, just out of reach, and make him generally uncomfortable, and they were so busy doing this that no one noticed that Blacky was not joining in the fun, and no one paid any attention to the old tumble-down nest of Redtail the Hawk only a few trees distant. So far Blacky's plans were working out just as he had hoped.

VI. Hooty the Owl Doesn't Stay Still

Now what's the good of being smart
When others do not do their part?

IF BLACKY the Crow didn't say this to himself, he
thought it. He knew that he had made a very cunning
plan to get the eggs of Hooty the Owl, a plan so shrewd
and cunning that no one else in the Green Forest or on the
Green Meadows would have thought of it. There was only
one weakness in it, and that was that it depended for success on having Hooty the Owl do as he usually did when
tormented by a crowd of noisy Crows,—stay where he
was until they got tired and flew away.

Now Blacky sometimes makes a mistake that smart people are very apt to make; he thinks that because he is so
smart, other people are stupid. That is where he proves
that smart as he is, he isn't as smart as he thinks he is. He
always thought of Hooty the Owl as stupid. That is, he always thought of him that way in daytime. At night, when
he was waked out of a sound sleep by the fierce hunting
cry of Hooty, he wasn't so sure about Hooty being stupid,
and he always took care to sit perfectly still in the dark-
ness, lest Hooty's great ears should hear him and Hooty's
great eyes, made for seeing in the dark, should find him.
No, in the night Blacky was not at all sure that Hooty was
stupid.

But in the daytime he was sure. You see, he quite forgot
the fact that the brightness of day is to Hooty what the
blackness of night is to him. So, because Hooty would simply sit still and hiss and snap his bill, instead of trying to
catch his tormentors or flying away, Blacky called him

stupid. He felt sure that Hooty would stay right where he was now, and he hoped that Mrs. Hooty would lose her temper and leave the nest where she was sitting on those two eggs and join Hooty to help him try to drive away that noisy crew.

But Hooty isn't stupid. Not a bit of it. The minute he found out that Blacky and his friends had discovered him, he thought of Mrs. Hooty and the two precious eggs in the old nest of Redtail the Hawk close by.

"Mrs. Hooty mustn't be disturbed," thought he. "That will never do at all. I must lead these black rascals away where they won't discover Mrs. Hooty. I certainly must."

So he spread his broad wings and blundered away among the trees a little way. He didn't fly far because the instant he started to fly that whole noisy crew with the exception of Blacky was after him. Because he couldn't use his claws or bill while flying, they grew bold enough to pull a few feathers out of his back. So he flew only a little way to a thick hemlock-tree, where it wasn't easy for the Crows to get at him, and where the light didn't hurt his eyes so much. There he rested a few minutes and then did the same thing over again. He meant to lead those bothersome Crows into the darkest part of the Green Forest and there—well, he could see better there, and it might be that one of them would be careless enough to come within reach. No, Hooty wasn't stupid. Certainly not.

Blacky awoke to that fact as he sat in the top of a tall pine-tree silently watching. He could see Mrs. Hooty on the nest, and as the noise of Hooty's tormentors sounded from farther and farther away, she settled herself more comfortably and closed her eyes. Blacky could imagine that she was smiling to herself. It was clear that she had no intention of going to help Hooty. His splendid plan had failed just because stupid Hooty, who wasn't stupid at all, had flown away when he ought to have sat still. It was very provoking.

VII. Blacky Tries Another Plan

When one plan fails, just try another;
Declare you'll win some way or other.

PEOPLE WHO succeed are those who do not give up because they fail the first time they try. They are the
ones who, as soon as one plan fails, get busy right away
and think of another plan and try that. If the thing they are
trying to do is a good thing, sooner or later they succeed.
If they are trying to do a wrong thing, very likely all their
plans fail, as they should.

Now Blacky the Crow knows all about the value of trying
and trying. He isn't easily discouraged. Sometimes it is a
pity that he isn't, because he plans so much mischief. But
the fact remains that he isn't, and he tries and tries until
he cannot think of another plan and just *has* to give up.
When he invited all his relatives to join him in tormenting
Hooty the Owl, he thought he had a plan that just couldn't
fail. He felt sure that Mrs. Hooty would leave her nest and
help Hooty try to drive away his tormentors. But Mrs.
Hooty didn't do anything of the kind, because Hooty was
smart enough and thoughtful enough to lead his tormentors away from the nest into the darkest part of the Green
Forest where their noise wouldn't bother Mrs. Hooty. So
she just settled herself more comfortably than ever on
those eggs which Blacky had hoped she would give him a
chance to steal, and his fine plan was quite upset.

Not one of his relatives had noticed that nest. They had
been too busy teasing Hooty. This was just as Blacky had
hoped. He didn't want them to know about that nest because
he was selfish and wanted to get those eggs just for himself

14

alone. But now he knew that the only way he could get Mrs. Hooty off of them would be by teasing her so that she would lose her temper and try to catch some of her tormentors. If she did that, there would be a chance that he might slip in and get at least one of those eggs. He would try it.

For a few minutes he listened to the noise of his relatives growing fainter and fainter, as Hooty led them farther and farther into the Green Forest. Then he opened his mouth.

"Caw, caw, caw, caw!" he screamed. "Caw, caw, caw, caw! Come back, everybody! Here is Mrs. Hooty on her nest! Caw, caw, caw, caw!"

Now as soon as they heard that, all Blacky's relatives stopped chasing and tormenting Hooty and started back as fast as they could fly. They didn't like the dark part of the Green Forest into which Hooty was leading them. Besides, they wanted to see that nest. So back they came, cawing at the top of their lungs, for they were very much excited. Some of them never had seen a nest of Hooty's. And anyway, it would be just as much fun to tease Mrs. Hooty as it was to tease Hooty.

"Where is the nest?" they screamed, as they came back to where Blacky was cawing and pretending to be very much excited.

"Why," exclaimed one, "that is the old nest of Redtail the Hawk. I know all about that nest." And he looked at Blacky as if he thought Blacky was playing a joke on them.

"It was Redtail's, but it is Hooty's now. If you don't believe me, just look in it," retorted Blacky.

At once they all began to fly over the top of the tree where they could look down into the nest and there, sure enough, was Mrs. Hooty, her great, round, yellow eyes glaring up at them angrily. Such a racket! Right away Hooty was forgotten, and the whole crowd at once began to torment Mrs. Hooty. Only Blacky sat watchful and silent, waiting for Mrs. Hooty to lose her temper and try to catch one of her tormentors. He had hope, a great hope, that he would get one of those eggs.

VIII. Hooty Comes to Mrs. Hooty's Aid

NO ONE CAN live just for self alone. A lot of people think they can, but they are very much mistaken. They are making one of the greatest mistakes in the world. Every teeny, weeny act, no matter what it is, affects somebody else. That is one of Old Mother Nature's great laws. And it is just as true among the little people of the Green Forest and the Green Meadows as with boys and girls and grown people. It is Old Mother Nature's way of making each of us responsible for the good of all and of teaching us that always we should help each other.

As you know, when Blacky the Crow called all his relatives over to the nest where Mrs. Hooty was sitting on her eggs, they at once stopped tormenting Hooty and left him alone in a thick hemlock-tree in the darkest part of the Green Forest. Of course Hooty was very, very glad to be left in peace, and he might have spent the rest of the day there sleeping in comfort. But he didn't. No, Sir, he didn't. At first he gave a great sigh of relief and settled himself as if he meant to stay. He listened to the voices of those noisy Crows growing fainter and fainter and was glad. But it was only for a few minutes. Presently those voices stopped growing fainter. They grew more excited-sounding than ever, and they came right from one place. Hooty knew then that his tormentors had found the nest where Mrs. Hooty was, and that they were tormenting her just as they had tormented him.

He snapped his bill angrily and then more angrily.

"I guess Mrs. Hooty is quite able to take care of herself," he grumbled, "but she ought not to be disturbed while she is sitting on those eggs. I hate to go back there in that

16

bright sunshine. It hurts my eyes, and I don't like it, but I guess I'll have to go back there. Mrs. Hooty needs my help. I'd rather stay here, but—"

He didn't finish. Instead, he spread his broad wings and flew back towards the nest and Mrs. Hooty. His great wings made no noise, for they are made so that he can fly without making a sound. "If I once get hold of one of those Crows!" he muttered to himself. "If I once get hold of one of those Crows, I'll—" He didn't say what he would do, but if you had been near enough to hear the snap of his bill, you could have guessed the rest.

All this time the Crows were having what they called fun with Mrs. Hooty. Nothing is true fun which makes others uncomfortable, but somehow a great many people seem to forget this. So, while Blacky sat watching, his relatives made a tremendous racket around Mrs. Hooty, and the more angry she grew, the more they screamed and called her names and darted down almost in her face, as they pretended that they were going to fight her. They were so busy doing this, and Blacky was so busy watching them, hoping that Mrs. Hooty would leave her nest and give him a chance to steal the eggs he knew were under her, that no one gave Hooty a thought.

All of a sudden he was there, right in the tree close to the nest! No one had heard a sound, but there he was, and in the claws of one foot he held the tail feathers of one of Blacky's relatives. It was lucky, very lucky indeed for that one that the sun was in Hooty's eyes and so he had missed his aim. Otherwise there would have been one less Crow.

Now it is one thing to tease one lone Owl and quite another to tease two together. Besides, there were those black tail feathers floating down to the snow-covered ground. Quite suddenly those Crows decided that they had had fun enough for one day, and in spite of all Blacky could do to stop them, away they flew, cawing loudly and talking it all over noisily. Blacky was the last to go, and his heart was sorrowful. However could he get those eggs?

All of a sudden he was there, right in the tree close to the nest!
Page 17

IX. Blacky Thinks of Farmer Brown's Boy

SUCH LUCK!" grumbled Blacky, as he flew over to his favorite tree to do a little thinking. "Such luck! Now all my neighbors know about the nest of Hooty the Owl, and sooner or later one of them will find out that there are eggs in it. There is one thing about it, though, and that is that if I can't get them, nobody can. That is to say, none of my relatives can. I've tried every way I can think of, and those eggs are still there. My, my, my, how I would like one of them right now!"

Then Blacky the Crow did a thing which disappointed scamps often do,—began to blame the ones he was trying to wrong because his plans had failed. To have heard him talking to himself, you would have supposed that those eggs really belonged to him and that Hooty and Mrs. Hooty had cheated him out of them. Yes, Sir, that is what you would have thought if you could have heard him muttering to himself there in the tree-top. In his disappointment over not getting those eggs, he was so sorry for himself that he actually did feel that he was the one wronged,—that Hooty and Mrs. Hooty should have let him have those eggs.

Of course, that was absolute foolishness, but he made himself believe it just the same. At least, he pretended to believe it. And the more he pretended, the angrier he grew. This is often the way with people who try to wrong others. They grow angry with the ones they have tried to wrong. When at last Blacky had to confess to himself that he could think of no other way to get those eggs, he began to wonder if there was some way to make trouble for

19

Hooty and Mrs. Hooty. It was right then that he thought of
Farmer Brown's boy.

Blacky's eyes snapped. He remembered how, once upon
a time, Farmer Brown's boy had delighted to rob nests.
Blacky had seen him take the eggs from the nests of
Blacky's own relatives and from many other feathered
people. What he did with the eggs, Blacky had no idea.
Just now he didn't care. If Farmer Brown's boy would just
happen to find Hooty's nest, he would be sure to take
those eggs, and then he, Blacky, would feel better. He
would feel that he was even with Hooty.

Right away he began to try to think of some way to
bring Farmer Brown's boy over to the lonesome corner of
the Green Forest where Hooty's nest was. If he could once
get him there, he felt sure that Farmer Brown's boy would
see the nest and climb up to it, and then of course he
would take the eggs. If he couldn't have those eggs himself, the next best thing would be to see some one else get
them.

Dear me, dear me, such dreadful thoughts! I am afraid
that Blacky's heart was as black as his coat. And the worst
of it was, he seemed to get a lot of pleasure in his wicked
plans. Now right down in his heart he knew that they were
wicked plans, but he tried to make excuses to himself.

"Hooty the Owl is a robber," said he. "Everybody is
afraid of him. He lives on other people, and so far as I
know he does no good in the world. He is big and fierce,
and no one loves him. The Green Forest would be better
off without him. If those eggs hatch, there will be little
Owls to be fed, and they will grow up into big fierce Owls,
like their father and mother. So if I show Farmer Brown's
boy that nest and he takes those eggs, I will be doing a
kindness to my neighbors."

So Blacky talked to himself and tried to hush the still,
small voice down inside that tried to tell him that what he
was planning to do was really a dreadful thing. And all the
time he watched for Farmer Brown's boy.

X. Farmer Brown's Boy and Hooty

FARMER BROWN'S boy had taken it into his head to visit the Green Forest. It was partly because he hadn't anything else to do, and it was partly because now that it was very near the end of winter he wanted to see how things were there and if there were any signs of the coming of spring. Blacky the Crow saw him coming, and Blacky chuckled to himself. He had watched every day for a week for just this thing. Now he would tell Farmer Brown's boy about that nest of Hooty the Owl.

He flew over to the lonesome corner of the Green Forest where Hooty and Mrs. Hooty had made their home and at once began to caw at the top of his voice and pretend that he was terribly excited over something.

"Caw, caw, caw, caw, caw!" shouted Blacky. At once all his relatives within hearing hurried over to join him. They knew that he was tormenting Hooty, and they wanted to join in the fun. It wasn't long before there was a great racket going on over in that lonesome corner of the Green Forest.

Of course Farmer Brown's boy heard it. He stopped and listened. "Now I wonder what Blacky and his friends have found this time," said he. "Whenever they make a fuss like that, there is usually something to see there. I believe I'll go over and have a look."

So he turned in the direction of the lonesome corner of the Green Forest, and as he drew near, he moved very carefully, so as to see all that he could without frightening the Crows. He knew that as soon as they saw him, they would fly away, and that might alarm the one they were tormenting, for he knew enough of Crow ways to know

21

that when they were making such a noise as they were now making, they were plaguing some one.

Blacky was the first to see him because he was watching for him. But he didn't say anything until Farmer Brown's boy was so near that he couldn't help but see that nest and Hooty himself, sitting up very straight and snapping his bill angrily at his tormentors. Then Blacky gave the alarm, and at once all the Crows rose in the air and headed for the Green Meadows, cawing at the top of their lungs. Blacky went with them a little way. The first chance he got he dropped out of the flock and silently flew back to a place where he could see all that might happen at the nest of Hooty the Owl.

When Farmer Brown's boy first caught sight of the nest and saw the Crows darting down toward it and acting so excited, he was puzzled.

"That's an old nest of Redtail the Hawk," thought he. "I found that last spring. Now what can there be there to excite those Crows so?"

Then he caught sight of Hooty the Owl. "Ha, so that's it!" he exclaimed. "Those scamps have discovered Hooty and have been having no end of fun tormenting him. I wonder what he's doing there."

He no longer tried to keep out of sight, but walked right up to the foot of the tree, all the time looking up. Hooty saw him, but instead of flying away, he snapped his bill just as he had at the Crows and hissed.

"That's funny," thought Farmer Brown's boy. "If I didn't know that to be the old nest of Redtail the Hawk, and if it weren't still the tail-end of winter, I would think that was Hooty's nest."

He walked in a circle around the tree, looking up. Suddenly he gave a little start. Was that a tail sticking over the edge of the nest? He found a stick and threw it up. It struck the bottom of the nest, and out flew a great bird. It was Mrs. Hooty! Blacky the Crow chuckled.

XI. Farmer Brown's Boy Is Tempted

When you're tempted to do wrong
Is the time to prove you're strong.
Shut your eyes and clench each fist;
It will help you to resist.

WHEN A BIRD is found sitting on a nest, it is a pretty sure sign that that nest holds something worth while. It is a sign that that bird has set up housekeeping. So when Farmer Brown's boy discovered Mrs. Hooty sitting so close on the old nest of Redtail the Hawk, in the most lonesome corner of the Green Forest, he knew what it meant. Perhaps I should say that he knew what it ought to mean. It ought to mean that there were eggs in that nest.

But it was hard for Farmer Brown's boy to believe that. Why, spring had not come yet! There was still snow, and the Smiling Pool was still covered with ice. Who ever heard of birds nesting at this time of year? Certainly not Farmer Brown's boy. And yet Hooty the Owl and Mrs. Hooty were acting for all the world as feathered folks do act when they have eggs and are afraid that something is going to happen to them. It was very puzzling.

"That nest was built by Redtail the Hawk, and it hasn't even been repaired," muttered Farmer Brown's boy, as he stared up at it. "If Hooty and his wife have taken it for their home, they are mighty poor housekeepers. And if Mrs. Hooty has laid eggs this time of year, she must be crazy. I suppose the way to find out is to climb up there. It seems foolish, but I'm going to do it. Those Owls certainly act as if they are mighty anxious about something, and I'm going to find out what it is."

23

He looked at Hooty and Mrs. Hooty, at their hooked bills and great claws, and decided that he would take a stout stick along with him. He had no desire to feel these great claws. When he had found a stick to suit him, he began to climb the tree. Hooty and Mrs. Hooty snapped their bills and hissed fiercely. They drew nearer. Farmer Brown's boy kept a watchful eye on them. They looked so big and fierce that he was almost tempted to give up and leave them in peace. But he just *had* to find out if there was anything in that nest, so he kept on. As he drew near it, Mrs. Hooty swooped very near to him, and the snap of her bill made an ugly sound. He held his stick ready to strike and kept on.

The nest was simply a great platform of sticks. When Farmer Brown's boy reached it, he found that he could not get where he could look into it, so he reached over and felt inside. Almost at once his fingers touched something that made him tingle all over. It was an egg, a great big egg! There was no doubt about it. It was just as hard for him to believe as it had been for Blacky the Crow to believe, when he first saw those eggs. Farmer Brown's boy's fingers closed over that egg and took it out of the nest. Mrs. Hooty swooped very close, and Farmer Brown's boy nearly dropped the egg as he struck at her with his stick. Then Mrs. Hooty and Hooty seemed to lose courage and withdrew to a tree near by, where they snapped their bills and hissed.

Then Farmer Brown's boy looked at the prize in his hand. It was a big, dirty-white egg. His eyes shone. What a splendid prize to add to his collection of birds' eggs! It was the first egg of the Great Horned Owl, the largest of all Owls, that he ever had seen.

Once more he felt in the nest and found there was another egg there. "I'll take both of them," said he. "It's the first nest of Hooty's that I've ever found, and perhaps I'll never find another. Gee, I'm glad I came over here to find out what those Crows were making such a fuss about. I wonder if I can get these down without breaking them."

Just at that very minute he remembered something. He remembered that he had stopped collecting eggs. He remembered that he had resolved never to take another bird's egg.

"But this is different," whispered the tempter. "This isn't like taking the eggs of the little song birds."

XII. A Tree-Top Battle

As black is black and white is white,
So wrong is wrong and right is right.

THERE ISN'T any half way about it. A thing is wrong or
it is right, and that is all there is to it. But most people
have hard work to see this when they want very much to
do a thing that the still small voice way down inside tells
them isn't right. They try to compromise. To compromise
is to do neither one thing nor the other but a little of both.
But you can't do that with right and wrong. It is a queer
thing, but a half right never is as good as a whole right,
while a half wrong often, very often, is as bad as a whole
wrong.

Farmer Brown's boy, up in the tree by the nest of Hooty
the Owl in the lonesome corner of the Green Forest, was
fighting a battle. No, he wasn't fighting with Hooty or
Mrs. Hooty. He was fighting a battle right inside himself.
It was a battle between right and wrong. Once upon a
time he had taken great delight in collecting the eggs of
birds, in trying to see how many kinds he could get. Then
as he had come to know the little forest and meadow people better, he had seen that taking the eggs of birds is
very, very wrong, and he had stopped stealing them. He
had declared that never again would he steal an egg from
a bird.

But never before had he found a nest of Hooty the Owl.
Those two big eggs would add ever so much to his collection. "Take 'em," said a little voice inside. "Hooty is a
robber. You will be doing a kindness to the other birds by
taking them."

"Don't do it," said another little voice. "Hooty may be a robber, but he has a place in the Green Forest, or Old Mother Nature never would have put him here. It is just as much stealing to take his eggs as to take the eggs of any other bird. He has just as much right to them as Jenny Wren has to hers."

"Take one and leave one," said the first voice.

"That will be just as much stealing as if you took both," said the second voice. "Besides, you will be breaking your own word. You said that you never would take another egg."

"I didn't promise anybody but myself," declared Farmer Brown's boy right out loud. At the sound of his voice, Hooty and Mrs. Hooty, sitting in the next tree, snapped their bills and hissed louder than ever.

"A promise to yourself ought to be just as good as a promise to any one else. I don't wonder Hooty hisses at you," said the good little voice.

"Think how fine those eggs will look in your collection and how proud you will be to show them to the other fellows who never have found a nest of Hooty's," said the first little voice.

"And think how mean and small and cheap you'll feel every time you look at them," added the good little voice. "You'll get a lot more fun if you leave them to hatch out and then watch the little Owls grow up and learn all about their ways. Just think what a stout, brave fellow Hooty is to start housekeeping at this time of year, and how wonderful it is that Mrs. Hooty can keep these eggs warm and when they have hatched take care of the baby Owls before others have even begun to build their nests. Besides, wrong is wrong and right is right, always."

Slowly Farmer Brown's boy reached over the edge of the nest and put back the egg. Then he began to climb down the tree. When he reached the ground he went off a little way and watched. Almost at once Mrs. Hooty flew to the nest and settled down on the eggs, while Hooty mounted guard close by.

"I'm glad I didn't take 'em," said Farmer Brown's boy. "Yes, Sir, I'm glad I didn't take 'em."

As he turned back toward home, he saw Blacky the Crow flying over the Green Forest, and little did he guess how he had upset Blacky's plans.

XIII. Blacky Has a Change of Heart

BLACKY THE CROW isn't all black. No, indeed. His coat is black, and sometimes it seems as if his heart is all black, but this isn't so. It certainly seemed as if his heart was all black when he tried so hard to make trouble for Hooty the Owl. It would seem as if only a black heart could have urged him to try so hard to steal the eggs of Hooty and Mrs. Hooty, but this wasn't really so. You see, it didn't seem at all wrong to try to get those eggs. Blacky was hungry, and those eggs would have given him a good meal. He knew that Hooty wouldn't hesitate to catch him and eat him if he had the chance, and so it seemed to him perfectly right and fair to steal Hooty's eggs if he was smart enough to do so. And most of the other little people of the Green Forest and the Green Meadows would have felt the same way about it. You see, it is one of the laws of Old Mother Nature that each one must learn to look out for himself.

But when Blacky showed that nest of Hooty's to Farmer Brown's boy with the hope that Farmer Brown's boy would steal those eggs, there *was* blackness in his heart. He was doing something then which was pure meanness. He was just trying to make trouble for Hooty, to get even because Hooty had been too smart for him. He had sat in the top of a tall pine-tree where he could see all that happened, and he had chuckled wickedly as he had seen Farmer Brown's boy climb to Hooty's nest and take out an egg. He felt sure that he would take both eggs. He hoped so, anyway.

When he saw Farmer Brown's boy put the eggs back and climb down the tree without any, he had to blink his

eyes to make sure that he saw straight. He just couldn't
believe what he saw. At first he was dreadfully disappointed and angry. It looked very much as if he weren't
going to get even with Hooty after all. He flew over to his
favorite tree to think things over. Now sometimes it is a
good thing to sit by oneself and think things over. It gives
the little small voice deep down inside a chance to be
heard. It was just that way with Blacky now.

The longer he thought, the meaner his action in calling
Farmer Brown's boy looked. It was one thing to try to
steal those eggs himself, but it was quite another matter
to try to have them stolen by some one against whom
Hooty had no protection whatever.

"If it had been any one but Hooty, you would have done
your best to have kept Farmer Brown's boy away," said
the little voice inside. Blacky hung his head. He knew that
it was true. More than once, in fact many times, he had
warned other feathered folks when Farmer Brown's boy
had been hunting for their nests, and had helped to lead
him away.

At last Blacky threw up his head and chuckled, and this
time his chuckle was good to hear. "I'm glad that Farmer
Brown's boy didn't take those eggs," said he right out
loud. "Yes, sir, I'm glad. I'll never do such a thing as that
again. I'm ashamed of what I did; yet I'm glad I did it. I'm
glad because I've learned some things. I've learned that
Farmer Brown's boy isn't as much to be feared as he used
to be. I've learned that Hooty isn't as stupid as I thought
he was. I've learned that while it may be all right for us
people of the Green Forest to try to outwit each other we
ought to protect each other against common dangers.
And I've learned something I didn't know before, and that
is that Hooty the Owl is the very first of us to set up
housekeeping. Now I think I'll go hunt for an honest meal."
And he did.

XIV. Blacky Makes a Call

Judge no one by his style of dress;
Your ignorance you thus confess.
Blacky the Crow.

"CAW, CAW, caw, caw." There was no need of looking to see who that was. Peter Rabbit knew without looking. Mrs. Quack knew without looking. Just the same, both looked up. Just alighting in the top of a tall tree was Blacky the Crow. "Caw, caw, caw, caw," he repeated, looking down at Peter and Mrs. Quack and Mr. Quack and the six young Quacks. "I hope I am not interrupting any secret gossip."

"Not at all," Peter hastened to say. "Mrs. Quack was just telling me of the troubles and dangers in bringing up a young family in the Far North. How did you know the Quacks had arrived?"

Blacky chuckled hoarsely. "I didn't," said he. "I simply thought there might be something going on I didn't know about over here in the pond of Paddy the Beaver, so I came over to find out. Mr. Quack, you and Mrs. Quack are looking very fine this fall. And those handsome young Quacks, you don't mean to tell me that they are your children!"

Mrs. Quack nodded proudly. "They are," said she.

"You don't say so!" exclaimed Blacky, as if he were very much surprised, when all the time he wasn't surprised at all. "They are a credit to their parents. Yes, indeed, they are a credit to their parents. Never have I seen finer young Ducks in all my life. How glad the hunters with terrible guns will be to see them."

31

"I hope I am not interrupting any secret gossip."
Page 31

Mrs. Quack shivered at that and Blacky saw it. He chuckled softly. You know he dearly loves to make others uncomfortable. "I saw three hunters over on the edge of the Big River early this very morning," said he.

Mrs. Quack looked more anxious than ever. Blacky's sharp eyes noted this.

"That is why I came over here," he added kindly. "I wanted to give you warning."

"But you didn't know the Quacks were here!" spoke up Peter.

"True enough, Peter. True enough," replied Blacky, his eyes twinkling. "But I thought they might be. I had heard a rumor that those who go south are traveling earlier than usual this fall, so I knew I might find Mr. and Mrs. Quack over here any time now. Is it true, Mrs. Quack, that we are going to have a long, hard, cold winter?"

"That is what they say up in the Far North," replied Mrs. Quack. "And it is true that Jack Frost had started down earlier than usual. That is how it happens we are here now. But about those hunters over by the Big River, do you suppose they will come over here?" There was an anxious note in Mrs. Quack's voice.

"No," replied Blacky promptly. "Farmer Brown's boy won't let them. I know. I've been watching him and he has been watching those hunters. As long as you stay here, you will be safe. What a great world this would be if all those two-legged creatures were like Farmer Brown's boy."

"Wouldn't it!" cried Peter. Then he added, "I wish they were."

"You don't wish it half as much as I do," declared Mrs. Quack.

"Yet I can remember when he used to hunt with a terrible gun and was as bad as the worst of them," said Blacky.

"What changed him?" asked Mrs. Quack, looking interested.

"Just getting really acquainted with some of the little people of the Green Forest and the Green Meadows," replied Blacky. "He found them ready to meet him more than halfway in friendship and that some of them really are his best friends."

"And now he is their best friend," spoke up Peter.

Blacky nodded. "Right, Peter," said he. "That is why the Quacks are safe here and will be as long as they stay."

XV. Blacky Does a Little Looking About

Do not take the word of others
That things are or are not so
When there is a chance that you may
Find out for yourself and *know*.
                    Blacky the Crow.

BLACKY THE CROW is a shrewd fellow. He is one of the smartest and shrewdest of all the little people in the Green Forest and on the Green Meadows. Everybody knows it. And because of this, all his neighbors have a great deal of respect for him, despite his mischievous ways.

Of course, Blacky had noticed that Johnny Chuck had dug his house deeper than usual and had stuffed himself until he was fatter than ever before. He had noticed that Jerry Muskrat was making the walls of his house thicker than in other years, and that Paddy the Beaver was doing the same thing to his house. You know there is very little that escapes the sharp eyes of Blacky the Crow.

He had guessed what these things meant. "They think we are going to have a long, hard, cold winter," muttered Blacky to himself. "Perhaps they know, but I want to see some signs of it for myself. They may be only guessing. Anybody can do that, and one guess is as good as another."

Then he found Mr. and Mrs. Quack, the Mallard Ducks, and their children in the pond of Paddy the Beaver and remembered that they never had come down from their home in the Far North as early in the fall as this. Mrs. Quack explained that Jack Frost had already started

35

Johnny Chuck had stuffed himself until he was fatter than ever before.
Page 35

south, and so they had started earlier to keep well ahead
of him.

"Looks as if there may be something in this idea of a
long, hard, cold winter," thought Blacky, "but perhaps the
Quacks are only guessing, too. I wouldn't take their word
for it any more than I would the word of Johnny Chuck or
Jerry Muskrat or Paddy the Beaver. I'll look about a little."

So after warning the Quacks to remain in the pond of
Paddy the Beaver if they would be safe, Blacky bade them
good-by and flew away. He headed straight for the Green
Meadows and Farmer Brown's cornfield. A little of that
yellow corn would make a good breakfast.

When he reached the cornfield, Blacky perched on top
of a shock of corn, for it already had been cut and put in
shocks in readiness to be carted up to Farmer Brown's
barn. For a few minutes he sat there silent and motion-
less, but all the time his sharp eyes were making sure that
no enemy was hiding behind one of those brown shocks.
When he was quite certain that things were as safe as they
seemed, he picked out a plump ear of corn and began to
tear open the husks, so as to get at the yellow grains.

"Seems to me these husks are unusually thick," muttered Blacky, as he tore at them with his stout bill. "Don't
remember ever having seen them as thick as these. Wonder if it just happens to be so on this ear."

Then, as a sudden thought popped into his black head,
he left that ear and went to another. The husks of this
were as thick as those on the first. He flew to another
shock and found the husks there just the same. He tried a
third shock with the same result.

"Huh, they are all alike," said he. Then he looked
thoughtful and for a few minutes sat perfectly still like a
black statue. "They are right," said he at last. "Yes, Sir,
they are right." Of course he meant Johnny Chuck and
Jerry Muskrat and Paddy the Beaver and the Quacks. "I
don't know how they know it, but they are right; we are
going to have a long, hard, cold winter. I know it myself
now. I've found a sign. Old Mother Nature has wrapped

this corn in extra thick husks, and of course she has done it to protect it. She doesn't do things without a reason. We are going to have a cold winter, or my name isn't Blacky the Crow."

XVI. Blacky Finds Other Signs

A single fact may fail to prove you either right or wrong;
Confirm it with another and your proof will then be strong.
                                            Blacky the Crow.

AFTER HIS discovery that Old Mother Nature had
wrapped all the ears of corn in extra thick husks,
Blacky had no doubt in his own mind that Johnny Chuck
and Jerry Muskrat and Paddy the Beaver and the Quacks
were quite right in feeling that the coming winter would
be long, hard and cold. But Blacky long ago learned that it
isn't wise or wholly safe to depend altogether on one
thing.

"Old Mother Nature never does things by halves,"
thought Blacky, as he sat on the fence post on the Green
Meadows, thinking over his discovery of the thick husks
on the corn. "She wouldn't take care to protect the corn
that way and not do as much for other things. There must
be other signs, if I am smart enough to find them."

He lifted one black wing and began to set in order the
feathers beneath it. Suddenly he made a funny little hop
straight up.

"Well, I never!" he exclaimed, as he spread his wings to
regain his balance. "I never did!"

"Is that so?" piped a squeaky little voice. "If you say you
never did, I suppose you never did, though I want the
word of some one else before I will believe it. What is it
you never did?"

Blacky looked down. Peeping up at him from the brown
grass were two bright little eyes.

"Hello, Danny Meadow Mouse!" exclaimed Blacky. "I

39

haven't seen you for a long time. I've looked for you several times lately."

"I don't doubt it. I don't doubt it at all," squeaked Danny. "You'll never see me when you are looking for me. That is, you won't if I can help it. You won't if I see you first."

Blacky chuckled. He knew what Danny meant. When Blacky goes looking for Danny Meadow Mouse, it usually is in hope of having a Meadow Mouse dinner, and he knew that Danny knew this. "I've had my breakfast," said Blacky, "and it isn't dinner time yet."

"What is it you never did?" persisted Danny, in his squeaky voice.

"That was just an exclamation," explained Blacky. "I made a discovery that surprised me so I exclaimed right out."

"What was it?" demanded Danny.

"It was that the feathers of my coat are coming in thicker than I ever knew them to before. I hadn't noticed it until I started to set them in order a minute ago." He buried his bill in the feathers of his breast. "Yes, sir," said he in a muffled voice, "they are coming in thicker than I ever knew them to before. There is a lot of down around the roots of them. I am going to have the warmest coat I've ever had."

"Well, don't think you are the only one," retorted Danny. "My fur never was so thick at this time of year as it is now, and it is the same way with Nanny Meadow Mouse and all our children. I suppose you know what it means."

"What does it mean?" asked Blacky, just as if he didn't have the least idea, although he had guessed the instant he discovered those extra feathers.

"It means we are going to have a long, hard, cold winter, and Old Mother Nature is preparing us for it," replied Danny, quite as if he knew all about it. "You'll find that everybody who doesn't go south or sleep all winter has a thicker coat than usual. Hello! There is old Roughleg the

Hawk! He has come extra early this year. I think I'll go back
to warn Nanny."

Without another word Danny disappeared in the brown
grass. Again Blacky chuckled. "More signs," said he to
himself. "More signs. There isn't a doubt that we are going
to have a hard winter. I wonder if I can stand it or if I'd better go a little way south, where it will be warmer."

XVII. Blacky Watches a Queer Performance

> This much to me is very clear:
> A thing not understood is queer.
> *Blacky the Crow.*

BLACKY THE CROW may be right. Again he may not be. If he is right, it will account for a lot of the queer people in the world. They are not understood, and so they are queer. At least, that is what other people say, and never once think that perhaps they are the queer ones for not understanding.

But Blacky isn't like those people who are satisfied not to understand and to think other people and things queer. He does his best to understand. He waits and watches and uses those sharp eyes of his and those quick wits of his until at last usually he does understand.

The day of his discovery of Old Mother Nature's signs that the coming winter would be long, hard and cold, Blacky paid a visit to the Big River. Long ago he discovered that many things are to be seen on or beside the Big River, things not to be seen elsewhere. So there are few days in which he does not get over there.

As he drew near the Big River, he was very watchful and careful, was Blacky, for this was the season when hunters with terrible guns were abroad, and he had discovered that they were likely to be hiding along the Big River, hoping to shoot Mr. or Mrs. Quack or some of their relatives. So he was very watchful as he drew near the Big River, for he had learned that it was dangerous to pass too near a hunter with a terrible gun. More than once he had been shot at. But he had learned by these experiences. Oh, yes,

Blacky had learned. For one thing, he had learned to know a gun when he saw it. For another thing, he had learned just how far away one of these dreadful guns could be and still hurt the one it was pointed at, and to always keep just a little farther away. Also he had learned that a man or boy without a terrible gun is quite harmless, and he had learned that hunters with terrible guns are tricky and sometimes hide from those they seek to kill, so that in the dreadful hunting season it is best to look sharply before approaching any place.

On this afternoon, as he drew near the Big River, he saw a man who seemed to be very busy on the shore of the Big River, at a place where wild rice and rushes grew for some distance out in the water, for just there it was shallow far out from the shore. Blacky looked sharply for a terrible gun. But the man had none with him and therefore was not to be feared. Blacky boldly drew near until he was able to see what the man was doing.

Then Blacky's eyes stretched their widest and he almost cawed right out with surprise. The man was taking yellow corn from a bag, a handful at a time, and throwing it out in the water. Yes, Sir, that is what he was doing, scattering nice yellow corn among the rushes and wild rice in the water!

"That's a queer performance," muttered Blacky, as he watched. "What is he throwing perfectly good corn out in the water for? He isn't planting it, for this isn't the planting season. Besides, it wouldn't grow in the water, anyway. It is a shame to waste nice corn like that. What is he doing it for?"

Blacky flew over to a tree some distance away and alighted in the top of it to watch the queer performance. You know Blacky has very keen eyes and he can see a long distance. For a while the man continued to scatter corn and Blacky continued to wonder what he was doing it for. At last the man went away in a boat. Blacky watched him until he was out of sight. Then he spread his wings and slowly flew back and forth just above the rushes and wild rice, at the place where the man had been scattering the corn. He could see some of the yellow grains on the bottom. Presently he saw something else. "Ha!" exclaimed Blacky.

XVIII. Blacky Becomes Very Suspicious

Of things you do not understand, Beware!
They may be wholly harmless but—Beware!
You'll find the older that you grow
That only things and folks you know
Are fully to be trusted, so Beware!

Blacky the Crow.

THAT IS ONE of Blacky's wise sayings, and he lives up
to it. It is one reason why he has come to be regarded
by all his neighbors as one of the smartest of all who live
in the Green Forest and on the Green Meadows. He sel-
dom gets into any real trouble because he first makes sure
there is no trouble to get into. When he discovers something he does not understand, he is at once distrustful
of it.

As he watched a man scattering yellow corn in the
water from the shore of the Big River he at once became
suspicious. He couldn't understand why a man should
throw good corn among the rushes and wild rice in the
water, and because he couldn't understand, he at once
began to suspect that for no good purpose. When the man
left in a boat, Blacky slowly flew over the rushes where
the man had thrown the corn, and presently his sharp
eyes made a discovery that caused him to exclaim right
out.

What was it Blacky had discovered? Only a few feathers. No one with eyes less sharp than Blacky's would have
noticed them. And few would have given them a thought
if they had noticed them. But Blacky knew right away that
those were feathers from a Duck. He knew that a Duck, or
perhaps a flock of Ducks, had been resting or feeding in

45

there among those rushes, and that in moving about they had left those two or three downy feathers.

"Ha!" exclaimed Blacky. "Mr. and Mrs. Quack or some of their relatives have been here. It is just the kind of a place Ducks like. Also some Ducks like corn. If they should come back here and find this corn, they would have a feast, and they would be sure to come again. That man who scattered the corn here didn't have a terrible gun, but that doesn't mean that he isn't a hunter. He may come back again, and then he may have a terrible gun. I'm suspicious of that man. I am so. I believe he put that corn here for Ducks and I don't believe he did it out of the kindness of his heart. If it was Farmer Brown's boy I would know that all is well; that he was thinking of hungry Ducks, with few places where they can feed in safety, as they make the long journey from the Far North to the Sunny South. But it wasn't Farmer Brown's boy. I don't like the looks of it. I don't indeed. I'll keep watch of this place and see what happens."

All the way to his favorite perch in a certain big hemlock-tree in the Green Forest, Blacky kept thinking about that corn and the man who had seemed to be generous with it, and the more he thought, the more suspicious he became. He didn't like the looks of it at all.

"I'll warn the Quacks to keep away from there. I'll do it the very first thing in the morning," he muttered, as he prepared to go to sleep. "If they have any sense at all, they will stay in the pond of Paddy the Beaver. But if they should go over to the Big River, they would be almost sure to find that corn, and if they should once find it, they would keep going back for more. It may be all right, but I don't like the looks of it."

And still full of suspicions, Blacky went to sleep.

XIX. Blacky Makes More Discoveries

Little things you fail to see
May important prove to be.
Blacky the Crow.

ONE OF THE secrets of Blacky's success in life is the fact that he never fails to take note of little things. Long ago he learned that little things which in themselves seem harmless and not worth noticing may together prove the most important things in life. So, no matter how unimportant a thing may appear, Blacky examines it closely with those sharp eyes of his and remembers it.

The very first thing Blacky did, as soon as he was awake the morning after he discovered the man scattering corn in the rushes at a certain place on the edge of the Big River, was to fly over to the pond of Paddy the Beaver and again warn Mr. and Mrs. Quack to keep away from the Big River, if they and their six children would remain safe. Then he got some breakfast. He ate it in a hurry and flew straight over to the Big River to the place where he had seen that yellow corn scattered.

Blacky wasn't wholly surprised to find Dusky the Black Duck, own cousin to Mr. and Mrs. Quack the Mallard Ducks, with a number of his relatives in among the rushes and wild rice at the very place where that corn had been scattered. They seemed quite contented and in the best of spirits. Blacky guessed why. Not a single grain of that yellow corn could Blacky see. He knew the ways of Dusky and his relatives. He knew that they must have come in there just at dusk the night before and at once had found that corn. He knew that they would remain hiding there until frightened out, and that then they would spend the day in some little pond where they would not be likely to be disturbed or where at least no danger could approach them without being seen in plenty of time. There they would rest all day, and when the Black Shadows came creeping out from the Purple Hills, they would return to that place on the Big River to feed, for that is the time when they like best to hunt for their food.

Dusky looked up as Blacky flew over him, but Blacky said nothing, and Dusky said nothing. But if Blacky didn't use his tongue, he did use his eyes. He saw just on the edge of the shore what looked like a lot of small bushes growing close together on the very edge of the water. Mixed in with them were a lot of the brown rushes. They looked very harmless and innocent. But Blacky knew every foot of that shore along the Big River, and he knew that those bushes hadn't been there during the summer. He knew that they hadn't grown there.

He flew directly over them. Just back of them were a couple of logs. Those logs hadn't been there when he passed that way a few days before. He was sure of it.

"Ha!" exclaimed Blacky under his breath. "Those look to me as if they might be very handy, very handy indeed, for a hunter to sit on. Sitting there behind those bushes, he would be hidden from any Duck who might come in to look for nice yellow corn scattered out there among the rushes. It doesn't look right to me. No, Sir, it doesn't look right to me. I think I'll keep an eye on this place."

So Blacky came back to the Big River several times that day. The second time back he found that Dusky the Black Duck and his relatives had left. When he returned in the afternoon, he saw the same man he had seen there the afternoon before, and he was doing the same thing,—scattering yellow corn out in the rushes. And as before, he went away in a boat.

"I don't like it," muttered Blacky, shaking his black head. "I don't like it."

XX. Blacky Drops a Hint

When you see another's danger
Warn him though he be a stranger.
Blacky the Crow.

EVERY DAY for a week a man came in a boat to scatter corn in the rushes at a certain point along the bank of the Big River, and every day Blacky the Crow watched him and shook his black head and talked to himself and told himself that he didn't like it, and that he was sure that it was for no good purpose. Sometimes Blacky watched from a distance, and sometimes he flew right over the man. But never once did the man have a gun with him.

Every morning, very early, Blacky flew over there, and every morning he found Dusky the Black Duck and his flock in the rushes and wild rice at that particular place, and he knew that they had been there all night. He knew that they had come in there just at dusk the night before, to feast on the yellow corn the man had scattered there in the afternoon.

"It is no business of mine what those Ducks do," muttered Blacky to himself, "but as surely as my tail feathers are black, something is going to happen to some of them one of these days. That man may be fooling them, but he isn't fooling me. Not a bit of it. He hasn't had a gun with him once when I have seen him, but just the same he is a hunter. I feel it in my bones. He knows those silly Ducks come in here every night for that corn he puts out. He knows that after they have been here a few times and nothing has frightened them, they will be so sure that it is a safe place that they will not be the least bit suspicious. Then he

49

will hide behind those bushes he has placed close to the edge of the water and wait for them with his terrible gun. That is what he will do, or my name isn't Blacky."

Finally Blacky decided to drop a hint to Dusky the Black Duck. So the next morning he stopped for a call. "Good morning," said he, as Dusky swam in just in front of him. "I hope you are feeling as fine as you look."

"Quack, quack," replied Dusky. "When Blacky the Crow flatters, he hopes to gain something. What is it this time?"

"Not a thing," replied Blacky. "On my honor, not a thing. There is nothing for me here, though there seems to be plenty for you and your relatives, to judge by the fact that I find you in this same place every morning. What is it?"

"Corn," replied Dusky in a low voice, as if afraid some one might overhear him. "Nice yellow corn."

"Corn!" exclaimed Blacky, as if very much astonished. "How does corn happen to be way over here in the water?"

Dusky shook his head. "Don't ask me, for I can't tell you," said he. "I haven't the least idea. All I know is that every evening when we arrive, we find it here. How it gets here, I don't know, and furthermore I don't care. It is enough for me that it is here."

"I've seen a man over here every afternoon," said Blacky. "I thought he might be a hunter."

"Did he have a terrible gun?" asked Dusky suspiciously.

"No-o," replied Blacky.

"Then he isn't a hunter," declared Dusky, looking much relieved.

"But perhaps one of these days he will have one and will wait for you to come in for your dinner," suggested Blacky. "He could hide behind these bushes, you know."

"Nonsense," retorted Dusky, tossing his head. "There hasn't been a sign of danger here since we have been here. I know you, Blacky; you are jealous because we find plenty to eat here, and you find nothing. You are trying to scare us. But I'll tell you right now, you can't scare us away from such splendid eating as we have had here. So there!"

XXI. At Last Blacky Is Sure

Who for another conquers fear
Is truly brave, it is most clear.
Blacky the Crow.

IT WAS LATE in the afternoon, and Blacky the Crow was on his way to the Green Forest. As usual, he went around by the Big River to see if that man was scattering corn for the Ducks. He wasn't there. No one was to be seen along the bank of the Big River.

"He hasn't come to-day, or else he came early and has left," thought Blacky. And then his sharp eyes caught sight of something that made him turn aside and make straight for a certain tree, from the top of which he could see all that went on for a long distance. What was it Blacky saw? It was a boat coming down the Big River.

Blacky sat still and watched. Presently the boat turned in among the rushes, and a moment later a man stepped out on the shore. It was the same man Blacky had watched scatter corn in the rushes every day for a week. There wasn't the least doubt about it, it was the same man.

"Ha, ha!" exclaimed Blacky, and nearly lost his balance in his excitement. "Ha, ha! It is just as I thought!" You see Blacky's sharp eyes had seen that the man was carrying something, and that something was a gun, a terrible gun. Blacky knows a terrible gun as far as he can see it.

The hunter, for of course that is what he was, tramped along the shore until he reached the bushes which Blacky had noticed close to the water and which he knew had not grown there. The hunter looked out over the Big River.

Then he walked along where he had scattered corn the day before. Not a grain was to be seen. This seemed to please him. Then he went back to the bushes and sat down on a log behind them, his terrible gun across his knees.

"I was sure of it," muttered Blacky. "He is going to wait there for those Ducks to come in, and then something dreadful will happen. What terrible creatures these hunters are! They don't know what fairness is. No, Sir, they don't know what fairness is. He has put food there day after day, where Dusky the Black Duck and his flock would be sure to find it, and has waited until they have become so sure there is no danger that they are no longer suspicious. He knows they will feel so sure that all is safe that they will come in without looking for danger. Then he will fire that terrible gun and kill them without giving them any chance at all.

"Reddy Fox is a sly, clever hunter, but he wouldn't do a thing like that. Neither would Old Man Coyote or anybody else who wears fur or feathers. They might hide and try to catch some one by surprise. That is all right, because each of us is supposed to be on the watch for things of that sort. Oh, dear, what's to be done? It is time I was getting home to the Green Forest. The Black Shadows will soon come creeping out from the Purple Hills, and I must be safe in my hemlock-tree by then. I would be scared to death to be out after dark. Yet those Ducks ought to be warned. Oh, dear, what shall I do?"

Blacky peered over at the Green Forest and then over toward the Purple Hills, behind which jolly, round, red Mr. Sun would go to bed very shortly. He shivered as he thought of the Black Shadows that soon would come swiftly out from the Purple Hills across the Big River and over the Green Meadows. With them might come Hooty the Owl, and Hooty wouldn't object in the least to a Crow dinner. He wished he was in that hemlock-tree that very minute.

Then Blacky looked at the hunter with his terrible gun

and thought of what might happen, what would be almost sure to happen, unless those Ducks were warned. "I'll wait a little while longer," muttered Blacky, and tried to feel brave. But instead he shivered.

XXII. Blacky Goes Home Happy

No greater happiness is won
Than through a deed for others done.
Blacky the Crow.

BLACKY SAT in the top of a tree near the bank of the Big River and couldn't make up his mind what to do. He wanted to get home to the big, thick hemlock-tree in the Green Forest before dusk, for Blacky is afraid of the dark. That is, he is afraid to be out after dark.

"Go along home," said a voice inside him, "there is hardly time now for you to get there before the Black Shadows arrive. Don't waste any more time here. What may happen to those silly Ducks is no business of yours, and there is nothing you can do, anyway. Go along home."

"Wait a few minutes," said another little voice down inside him. "Don't be a coward. You ought to warn Dusky the Black Duck and his flock that a hunter with a terrible gun is waiting for them. Is it true that it is no business of yours what happens to those Ducks? Think again, Blacky; think again. It is the duty of each one who sees a common danger to warn his neighbors. If something dreadful should happen to Dusky because you were afraid of the dark, you never would be comfortable in your own mind. Stay a little while and keep watch."

Not five minutes later Blacky saw something that made him, oh, so glad he had kept watch. It was a swiftly moving black line just above the water far down the Big River, and it was coming up. He knew what that black line was. He looked over at the hunter hiding behind some bushes close to the edge of the water. The hunter was crouching

with his terrible gun in his hands and was peeping over
the bushes, watching that black line. He, too, knew what
it was. It was a flock of Ducks flying.

Blacky was all ashake again, but this time it wasn't with
fear of being caught away from home in the dark; it was
with excitement. He knew that those Ducks had become so
eager for more of that corn, that delicious yellow corn
which every night for a week they had found scattered in
the rushes just in front of the place where that hunter was
now hiding, that they couldn't wait for the coming of the
Black Shadows. They were so sure there was no danger
that they were coming in to eat without waiting for the
Black Shadows, as they usually did. And Blacky was glad.
Perhaps now he could give them warning.

Up the middle of the Big River, flying just above the
water, swept the flock with Dusky at its head. How swiftly
they flew, those nine big birds! Blacky envied them their
swift wings. On past the hidden hunter but far out over
the Big River they swept. For just a minute Blacky thought
they were going on up the river and not coming in to eat,
after all. Then they turned toward the other shore, swept
around in a circle and headed straight in toward that hidden hunter. Blacky glanced at him and saw that he was
ready to shoot.

Almost without thinking, Blacky spread his wings and
started out from that tree. "Caw, caw, caw, caw, caw!" he
shrieked at the top of his lungs. "Caw, caw, caw, caw, caw!"
It was his danger cry that everybody on the Green Meadows and in the Green Forest knows.

Instantly Dusky turned and began to climb up, up, up,
the other Ducks following him until, as they passed over
the hidden hunter, they were so high it was useless for
him to shoot. He did put up his gun and aim at them, but
he didn't shoot. You see, he didn't want to frighten them
so that they would not return. Then the flock turned and
started off in the direction from which they had come,
and in a few minutes they were merely a black line disap-
pearing far down the Big River.

Blacky headed straight for the Green Forest, chuckling as he flew. He knew that those Ducks would not return until after dark. He had saved them this time, and he was so happy he didn't even notice the Black Shadows. And the hunter stood up and shook his fist at Blacky the Crow.

XXIII. Blacky Calls Farmer Brown's Boy

BLACKY AWOKE in the best of spirits. Late the afternoon before he had saved Dusky the Black Duck and his flock from a hunter with a terrible gun. He wasn't quite sure whether he was most happy in having saved those Ducks by warning them just in time, or in having spoiled the plans of that hunter. He hates a hunter with a terrible gun, does Blacky. For that matter, so do all the little people of the Green Forest and the Green Meadows.

So Blacky started out for his breakfast in high spirits. After breakfast, he flew over to the Big River to see if Dusky the Black Duck was feeding in the rushes along the shore. Dusky wasn't, and Blacky guessed that he and his flock had been so frightened by that warning that they had kept away from there the night before.

"But they'll come back after a night or so," muttered Blacky, as he alighted in the top of a tree, the same tree from which he had watched the hunter the afternoon before. "They'll come back, and so will that hunter. If he sees me around again, he'll try to shoot me. I've done all I can do. Anyway, Dusky ought to have sense enough to be suspicious of this place after that warning. Hello, who is that? I do believe it is Farmer Brown's boy. I wish he would come over here. If he should find out about that hunter, perhaps he would do something to drive him away. I'll see if I can call him over here."

Blacky began to call in the way he does when he has discovered something and wants others to know about it. "Caw, caw, caaw, caaw, caw, caw, caaw!" screamed Blacky, as if greatly excited.

Now Farmer Brown's boy, having no work to do that

morning, had started for a tramp over the Green Meadows, hoping to see some of his little friends in feathers
and fur. He heard the excited cawing of Blacky and at once
turned in that direction.

"That black rascal has found something over on the
shore of the Big River," said Farmer Brown's boy to himself. "I'll go over there to see what it is. There isn't much
escapes the sharp eyes of that black busybody. He has led
me to a lot of interesting things, one time and another.
There he is on the top of that tree over by the Big River."

As Farmer Brown's boy drew near, Blacky flew down
and disappeared below the bank. Farmer Brown's boy
chuckled. "Whatever it is, it is right down there," he
muttered.

He walked forward rapidly but quietly, and presently he
reached the edge of the bank. Up flew Blacky cawing
wildly, and pretending to be scared half to death. Again
Farmer Brown's boy chuckled. "You're just making believe," he declared. "You're trying to make me believe that
I have surprised you, when all the time you knew I was
coming and have been waiting for me. Now, what have
you found over here?"

He looked eagerly along the shore, and at once he saw
a row of low bushes close to the edge of the water. He
knew what it was instantly. "A Duck blind!" he exclaimed.
"A hunter has built a blind over here from which to shoot
Ducks. I wonder if he has killed any yet. I hope not."

He went down to the blind, for that is what a Duck
hunter's hiding-place is called, and looked about. A couple
of grains of corn just inside the blind caught his eyes, and
his face darkened. "That fellow has been baiting Ducks,"
thought he. "He has been putting out corn to get them to
come here regularly. My, how I hate that sort of thing! It is
bad enough to hunt them fairly, but to feed them and then
kill them—ugh! I wonder if he has shot any yet."

He looked all about keenly, and his face cleared. He
knew that if that hunter had killed any Ducks, there would
be tell-tale feathers in the blind, and there were none.

XXIV. Farmer Brown's Boy
Does Some Thinking

FARMER BROWN'S BOY sat on the bank of the Big River in a brown study. That means that he was thinking very hard. Blacky the Crow sat in the top of a tall tree a short distance away and watched him. Blacky was silent now, and there was a knowing look in his shrewd little eyes. In calling Farmer Brown's boy over there, he had done all he could, and he was quite satisfied to leave the matter to Farmer Brown's boy.

"A hunter has made that blind to shoot Black Ducks from," thought Farmer Brown's boy, "and he has been baiting them in here by scattering corn for them. Black Ducks are about the smartest Ducks that fly, but if they have been coming in here every evening and finding corn and no sign of danger, they probably think it perfectly safe here and come straight in without being at all suspicious. To-night, or some night soon, that hunter will be waiting for them.

"I guess the law that permits hunting Ducks is all right, but there ought to be a law against baiting them in. That isn't hunting. No, Sir, that isn't hunting. If this land were my father's, I would know what to do. I would put up a sign saying that this was private property and no shooting was allowed. But it isn't my father's land, and that hunter has a perfect right to shoot here. He has just as much right here as I have. I wish I could stop him, but I don't see how I can."

A frown puckered the freckled face of Farmer Brown's boy. You see, he was thinking very hard, and when he does that he is very apt to frown.

"I suppose," he muttered, "I can tear down his blind. He wouldn't know who did it. But that wouldn't do much good; he would build another. Besides, it wouldn't be right. He has a perfect right to make a blind here, and having made it, it is his and I haven't any right to touch it. I won't do a thing I haven't a right to do. That wouldn't be honest. I've got to think of some other way of saving those Ducks."

The frown on his freckled face grew deeper, and for a long time he sat without moving. Suddenly his face cleared, and he jumped to his feet. He began to chuckle. "I have it!" he exclaimed. "I'll do a little shooting myself!" Then he chuckled again and started for home. Presently he began to whistle, a way he has when he is in good spirits.

Blacky the Crow watched him go, and Blacky was well satisfied. He didn't know what Farmer Brown's boy was planning to do, but he had a feeling that he was planning to do something, and that all would be well. Perhaps Blacky wouldn't have felt so sure could he have understood what Farmer Brown's boy had said about doing a little shooting himself.

As it was, Blacky flew off about his own business, quite satisfied that now all would be well, and he need worry no more about those Ducks. None of the little people of the Green Forest and the Green Meadows knew Farmer Brown's boy better than did Blacky the Crow. None knew better than he that Farmer Brown's boy was their best friend.

"It is all right now," chuckled Blacky. "It is all right now." And as the cheery whistle of Farmer Brown's boy floated back to him on the Merry Little Breezes, he repeated it: "It is all right now."

XXV. Blacky Gets a Dreadful Shock

When friends prove false, whom may we trust?
The springs of faith are turned to dust.
Blacky the Crow.

BLACKY THE CROW was in the top of his favorite tree
over near the Big River early this afternoon. He didn't
know what was going to happen, but he felt in his bones
that something was, and he meant to be on hand to see.
For a long time he sat there, seeing nothing unusual. At
last he spied a tiny figure far away across the Green Meadows. Even at that distance he knew who it was; it was
Farmer Brown's boy, and he was coming toward the Big
River.

"I thought as much," chuckled Blacky. "He is coming
over here to drive that hunter away."

The tiny figure grew larger. It was Farmer Brown's boy
beyond a doubt. Suddenly Blacky's eyes opened so wide
that they looked as if they were in danger of popping out
of his head. He had discovered that Farmer Brown's boy
was carrying something and that that something was a
gun! Yes, Sir, Farmer Brown's boy was carrying a terrible
gun! If Blacky could have rubbed his eyes, he would have
done so, just to make sure that there was nothing the matter with them.

"A gun!" croaked Blacky. "Farmer Brown's boy with a
terrible gun! What does it mean?"

Nearer came Farmer Brown's boy, and Blacky could see
that terrible gun plainly now. Suddenly an idea popped
into his head. "Perhaps he is going to shoot that hunter!"
thought Blacky, and somehow he felt better.

Farmer Brown's boy reached the Big River at a point some distance below the blind built by the hunter. He laid his gun down on the bank and went down to the edge of the water. The rushes grew very thick there, and for a while Farmer Brown's boy was very busy among them. Blacky from his high perch could watch him, and as he watched, he grew more and more puzzled. It looked very much as if Farmer Brown's boy was building a blind much like that of the hunter's. At last he carried an old log down there, got his gun, and sat down just as the hunter had done in his blind the afternoon before. He was quite hidden there, excepting from a place high up like Blacky's perch.

"I—I—I do believe he is going to try to shoot those Ducks himself," gasped Blacky. "I wouldn't have believed it if any one had told me. No, Sir, I wouldn't have believed it. I—I—can't believe it now. Farmer Brown's boy hunting with a terrible gun! Yet I've got to believe my own eyes."

A noise up river caught his attention. It was the noise of oars in a boat. There was the hunter, rowing down the Big River. Just as he had done the day before, he came ashore above his blind and walked down to it.

"This is no place for me," muttered Blacky. "He'll remember that I scared those Ducks yesterday, and as likely as not he'll try to shoot me."

Blacky spread his black wings and hurriedly left the tree-top, heading for another tree farther back on the Green Meadows where he would be safe, but from which he could not see as well. There he sat until the Black Shadows warned him that it was high time for him to be getting back to the Green Forest.

He had to hurry, for it was later than usual, and he was afraid to be out after dark. Just as he reached the Green Forest he heard a faint "bang, bang" from over by the Big River, and he knew that it came from the place where Farmer Brown's boy was hiding in the rushes.

"It is true," croaked Blacky. "Farmer Brown's boy has turned hunter." It was such a dreadful shock to Blacky that it was a long time before he could go to sleep.

XXVI. Why the Hunter Got No Ducks

THE HUNTER who had come down the Big River in a boat and landed near the place where Dusky the Black Duck and his flock had found nice yellow corn scattered in the rushes night after night saw Blacky the Crow leave the top of a certain tree as he approached.

"It is well for you that you didn't wait for me to get nearer," said the hunter. "You are smart enough to know that you can't play the same trick on me twice. You frightened those Ducks away last night, but if you try it again, you'll be shot as surely as your coat is black."

Then the hunter went to his blind which, you know, was the hiding-place he had made of bushes and rushes, and behind this he sat down with his terrible gun to wait and watch for Dusky the Black Duck and his flock.

Now you remember that farther along the shore of the Big River was Farmer Brown's boy, hiding in a blind he had made that afternoon. The hunter couldn't see him at all. He didn't have the least idea that any one else was anywhere near. "With that Crow out of the way, I think I will get some Ducks to-night," thought the hunter and looked at his gun to make sure that it was ready.

Over in the West, jolly, round, red Mr. Sun started to go to bed behind the Purple Hills, and the Black Shadows came creeping out. Far down the Big River the hunter saw a swiftly moving black line just above the water. "Here they come," he muttered, as he eagerly watched that black line draw nearer.

Twice those big black birds circled around over the Big River opposite where the hunter was crouching behind his blind. It was plain that Dusky, their leader, remembered

Blacky's warning the night before. But this time there was no warning. Everything appeared safe. Once more the flock circled and then headed straight for that place where they hoped to find more corn. The hunter crouched lower. They were almost near enough for him to shoot when "bang, bang" went a gun a short distance away.

Instantly Dusky and his flock turned and on swift wings swung off and up the river. If ever there was a disappointed hunter, it was the one crouching in that blind. "Somebody else is hunting, and he spoiled my shot that time," he muttered. "He must have a blind farther down. Probably some other Ducks I didn't see came in to him. I wonder if he got them. Here's hoping that next time those Ducks come in here first."

He once more made himself comfortable and settled down for a long wait. The Black Shadows crept out from the farther bank of the Big River. Jolly, round red Mr. Sun had gone to bed, and the first little star was twinkling high overhead. It was very still and peaceful. From out in the middle of the Big River sounded a low "quack"; Dusky and his flock were swimming in this time. Presently the hunter could see a silver line on the water, and then he made out nine black spots. In a few minutes those Ducks would be where he could shoot them.

"Bang, bang" went that gun below him again. With a roar of wings, Dusky and his flock were in the air and away. That hunter stood up and said things, and they were not nice things. He knew that those Ducks would not come back again that night, and that once more he must go home empty-handed. But first he would find out who that other hunter was and what luck he had had, so he tramped down the shore to where that gun had seemed to be. He found the blind of Farmer Brown's boy, but there was no one there. You see, as soon as he had fired his gun the last time, Farmer Brown's boy had slipped out and away. And as he tramped across the Green Meadows toward home with his gun, he chuckled. "He didn't get those Ducks this time," said Farmer Brown's boy.

XXVII. The Hunter Gives Up

BLACKY THE CROW didn't know what to think. He couldn't make himself believe that Farmer Brown's boy had really turned hunter, yet what else could he believe? Hadn't he with his own eyes seen Farmer Brown's boy with a terrible gun hide in rushes along the Big River and wait for Dusky the Black Duck and his flock to come in? And hadn't he with his own ears heard the "bang, bang" of that very gun?

The very first thing the next morning Blacky had hastened over to the place where Farmer Brown's boy had hidden in the rushes. With sharp eyes he looked for feathers, that would tell the tale of a Duck killed. But there were no feathers. There wasn't a thing to show that anything so dreadful had happened. Perhaps Farmer Brown's boy had missed when he shot at those Ducks. Blacky shook his head and decided to say nothing to anybody about Farmer Brown's boy and that terrible gun.

You may be sure that early in the afternoon he was perched in the top of his favorite tree over by the Big River. His heart sank, just as on the afternoon before, when he saw Farmer Brown's boy with his terrible gun trudging across the Green Meadows to the Big River. Instead of going to the same hiding place he made a new one farther down.

Then came the hunter a little earlier than usual. Instead of stopping at his blind, he walked straight to the blind Farmer Brown's boy had first made. Of course, there was no one there. The hunter looked both glad and disappointed. He went back to his own blind and sat down, and while he watched for the coming of the Ducks, he also

watched that other blind to see if the unknown hunter of
the night before would appear. Of course he didn't, and
when at last the hunter saw the Ducks coming, he was
sure that this time he would get some of them.

But the same thing happened as on the night before.
Just as those Ducks were almost near enough, a gun went
"bang, bang," and away went the Ducks. They didn't come
back again, and once more a disappointed hunter went
home without any.

The next afternoon he was on hand very early. He was
there before Farmer Brown's boy arrived, and when he
did come, of course the hunter saw him. He walked down
to where Farmer Brown's boy was hiding in the rushes.
"Hello!" said he. "Are you the one who was shooting here
last night and the night before?"

Farmer Brown's boy grinned. "Yes," said he.

"What luck did you have?" asked the hunter.

"Fine," replied Farmer Brown's boy.

"How many Ducks did you get?" asked the hunter.

Farmer Brown's boy grinned more broadly than before.
"None," said he. "I guess I'm not a very good shot."

"Then what did you mean by saying you had fine luck?"
demanded the hunter.

"Oh," replied Farmer Brown's boy, "I had the luck to see
those Ducks and the fun of shooting," and he grinned
again.

The hunter lost patience. He tried to order Farmer
Brown's boy away. But the latter said he had as much
right there as the hunter had, and the hunter knew that
this was so. Finally he gave up, and muttering angrily, he
went back to his blind. Again the gun of Farmer Brown's
boy frightened away the Ducks just as they were coming
in.

The next afternoon there was no hunter nor the next,
though Farmer Brown's boy was there. The hunter had
decided that it was a waste of time to hunt there while
Farmer Brown's boy was about.

XXVIII. Blacky Has a Talk with Dusky the Black Duck

Doubt not a friend, but to the last
Grip hard on faith and hold it fast.
Blacky the Crow.

EVERY MORNING Blacky the Crow visited the rushes along the shore of the Big River, hoping to find Dusky the Black Duck. He was anxious, was Blacky. He feared that Dusky or some of his flock had been killed, and he wanted to know. You see, he knew that Farmer Brown's boy had been shooting over there. At last, early one morning, he found Dusky and his flock in the rushes and wild rice. Eagerly he counted them. There were nine. Not one was missing. Blacky sighed with relief and dropped down on the shore close to where Dusky was taking a nap.

"Hello!" said Blacky.

Dusky awoke with a start. "Hello, yourself," said he.

"I've heard a terrible gun banging over here, and I was afraid you or some of your flock had been shot," said Blacky.

"We haven't lost a feather," declared Dusky. "That gun wasn't fired at us, anyway."

"Then who was it fired at?" demanded Blacky.

"I haven't the least idea," replied Dusky.

"Have you seen any other Ducks about here?" inquired Blacky.

"Not one," was Dusky's prompt reply. "If there had been any, I guess we would have known it."

"Did you know that when that terrible gun was fired

67

there was another terrible gun right over behind those bushes?" asked Blacky.

Dusky shook his head. "No," said he, "but I learned long ago that where there is one terrible gun there is likely to be more, and so when I heard that one bang, I led my flock away from here in a hurry. We didn't want to take any chances."

"It is a lucky thing you did," replied Blacky. "There was a hunter hiding behind those bushes all the time. I warned you of him once."

"That reminds me that I haven't thanked you," said Dusky. "I knew there was something wrong over here, but I didn't know what. So it was a hunter. I guess it is a good thing that I heeded your warning."

"I guess it is," retorted Blacky dryly. "Do you come here in daytime instead of night now?"

"No," replied Dusky. "We come in after dark and spend the night here. There is nothing to fear from hunters after dark. We've given up coming here until late in the evening. And since we did that, we haven't heard a gun."

Blacky gossiped a while longer, then flew off to look for his breakfast; and as he flew his heart was light. His shrewd little eyes twinkled.

"I ought to have known Farmer Brown's boy better than even to suspect him," thought he. "I know now why he had that terrible gun. It was to frighten those Ducks away so that the hunter would not have a chance to shoot them. He wasn't shooting at anything. He just fired in the air to scare those Ducks away. I know it just as well as if I had seen him do it. I'll never doubt Farmer Brown's boy again. And I'm glad I didn't say a word to anybody about seeing him with a terrible gun."

Blacky was right. Farmer Brown's boy had taken that way of making sure that the hunter who had first baited those Ducks with yellow corn scattered in the rushes in front of his hiding place should have no chance to kill any of them. While appearing to be an enemy, he really had been a friend of Dusky the Black Duck and his flock.

XXIX. Blacky Discovers an Egg

BLACKY IS FOND of eggs, as you know. In this he is a great deal like other people, Farmer Brown's boy for instance. But as Blacky cannot keep hens, as Farmer Brown's boy does, he is obliged to steal eggs or else go without. If you come right down to plain, everyday truth, I suppose Blacky isn't so far wrong when he insists that he is no more of a thief than Farmer Brown's boy. Blacky says that the eggs which the hens lay belong to the hens, and that he, Blacky has just as much right to take them as Farmer Brown's boy. He quite overlooks the fact that Farmer Brown's boy feeds the biddies and takes the eggs as pay. Anyway, that is what Farmer Brown's boy says, but I do not know whether or not the biddies understand it that way.

So Blacky the Crow cannot see why he should not help himself to an egg when he gets the chance. He doesn't get the chance very often to steal eggs from the hens, because usually they lay their eggs in the henhouse, and Blacky is too suspicious to venture inside. The eggs he does get are mostly those of his neighbors in the Green Forest and the Old Orchard. But once in a great while some foolish hen will make a nest outside the henhouse somewhere, and if Blacky happens to find it the black scamp watches every minute he can spare from other mischief for a chance to steal an egg.

Now Blacky knows just what a rogue Farmer Brown's boy thinks he is, and for this reason Blacky is very careful about approaching Farmer Brown or any other man until he has made sure that he runs no risk of being shot. Blacky knows quite as well as any one what a gun looks

69

like. He also knows that without a terrible gun, there is little Farmer Brown or any one else can do to him. So when
he sees Farmer Brown out in his fields, Blacky often will
fly right over him and shout "Caw, caw, caw, ca-a-w!" in the
most provoking way, and Farmer Brown's boy insists that
he has seen Blacky wink when he was doing it.

But Blacky doesn't do anything of this kind around the
buildings of Farmer Brown. You see, he has learned that
there are doors and windows in buildings, and out of one
of these a terrible gun may bang at any time. Though he
has suspected that Farmer Brown's boy would not now
try to harm him, Blacky is naturally cautious and takes no
chances. So when he comes spying around Farmer
Brown's house and barn, he does it when he is quite sure
that no one is about, and he makes no noise about it. First
he sits in a tall tree from which he can watch Farmer
Brown's home. When he is quite sure that the way is clear,
he flies over to the Old Orchard, and from there he in-
spects the barnyard, never once making a sound. If he is
quite sure that no one is about, he sometimes drops down
into the henyard and helps himself to corn, if any happens
to be there.

It was on one of those silent visits that Blacky spied
something which he couldn't forget. It was a box just inside the henhouse door. In the box was some hay and in
that hay he was sure that he had seen an egg. In fact, he
was sure that he saw two eggs there. He might not have
noticed them but for the fact that a hen had jumped down
from that box, making a terrible fuss. She didn't seem
frightened, but very proud. What under the sun she had
to be proud about Blacky couldn't understand, but he
didn't stay to find out. The noise she was making made
him nervous. He was afraid that it would bring some one
to find out what was going on. So he spread his black
wings and flew away as silently as he had come.

As he was flying away he saw those eggs. You see, as he
rose into the air, he managed to pass that open door in
such a way that he could glance in. That one glance was

enough. You know Blacky's eyes are very sharp. He saw the hay in the box and the two eggs in the hay, and that was enough for him. From that instant Blacky the Crow began to scheme and plan to get one or both of those eggs. It seemed to him that he never, never, had wanted anything quite so much, and he was sure that he would not and could not be happy until he succeeded in getting one.

XXX. Blacky Screws Up His Courage

IF OUT OF SIGHT, then out of mind. This is a saying which you often hear. It may be true sometimes, but it is very far from true at other times. Take the case of Blacky. He had had only a glance into that nest just inside the door of Farmer Brown's henhouse, but that glance had been enough to show him two eggs there. Then, as he flew away toward the Green Forest, those eggs were out of sight, of course. But do you think they were out of mind? Not much! No, indeed! In fact, those eggs were very much in Blacky's mind. He couldn't think of anything else. He flew straight to a certain tall pine-tree in a lonely part of the Green Forest. Whenever Blacky wants to think or to plan mischief, he seeks that particular tree, and in the shelter of its broad branches he keeps out of sight of curious eyes, and there he sits as still as still can be.

"I want one of those eggs," muttered Blacky, as he settled himself in comfort on a certain particular spot on a certain particular branch of that tall pine-tree. Indeed, that particular branch might well be called the "mischief branch," for on it Blacky has thought out and planned most of the mischief he is so famous for. "Yes, sir," he continued, "I want one of those eggs, and what is more, I am going to have one."

He half closed his eyes and tipped his head back and swallowed a couple of times, as if he already tasted one of those eggs.

"There is more in one of those eggs than in a whole nestful of Welcome Robin's eggs. It is a very long time since I have been lucky enough to taste a hen's egg, and now is my chance. I don't like having to go inside that

72

henhouse, even though it is barely inside the door. I'm
suspicious of doors. They have a way of closing most un-
expectedly. I might see if I cannot get Unc' Billy Possum to
bring one of those eggs out for me. But that plan won't do,
come to think of it, because I can't trust Unc' Billy. The old
sinner is too fond of eggs himself. I would be willing to di-
vide with him, but he would be sure to eat his first, and I
fear that it would taste so good that he would eat the
other. No. I've got to get one of those eggs myself. It is the
only way I can be sure of it.

"The thing to do is to make sure that Farmer Brown's
boy and Farmer Brown himself are nowhere about. They
ought to be down in the cornfield pretty soon. With them
down there, I have only to watch my chance and slip in. It
won't take but a second. Just a little courage, Blacky, just
a little courage! Nothing in this world worth having is
gained without some risk. The thing to do is to make sure
that the risk is as small as possible."

Blacky shook out his feathers and then flew out of the
tall pine-tree as silently as he had flown into it. He headed
straight toward Farmer Brown's cornfield. When he was
near enough to see all over the field, he dropped down to
the top of a fence post, and there he waited. He didn't
have long to wait. In fact, he had been there but a few minutes when he spied two people coming down the Long
Lane toward the cornfield. He looked at them sharply, and
then gave a little sigh of satisfaction. They were Farmer
Brown and Farmer Brown's boy. Presently they reached
the cornfield and turned into it. Then they went to work,
and Blacky knew that so far as they were concerned, the
way was clear for him to visit the henyard.

He didn't fly straight there. Oh, my, no! Blacky is too
clever to do anything like that. He flew toward the Green
Forest. When he knew that he was out of sight of those in
the cornfield, he turned and flew over to the Old Orchard,
and from the top of one of the old apple-trees he studied
the henyard and the barnyard and Farmer Brown's house
and the barn, to make absolutely sure that there was no

danger near. When he was quite sure, he silently flew
down into the henyard as he had done many times before.
He pretended to be looking for scattered grains of corn,
but all the time he was edging nearer and nearer to the
open door of the henhouse. At last he could see the box
with the hay in it. He walked right up to the open door and
peered inside. There was nothing to be afraid of that he
could see. Still he hesitated. He did hate to go inside that
door, even for a minute, and that is all it would take to fly
up to that nest and get one of those eggs.

Blacky closed his eyes for just a second, and when he
did that he seemed to see himself eating one of those
eggs. "What are you afraid of?" he muttered to himself as
he opened his eyes. Then with a hurried look in all direc-
tions, he flew up to the edge of the box. There lay the two
eggs!

XXXI. An Egg That Wouldn't Behave

If you had an egg and it wouldn't behave
Just what would you do with that egg, may I ask?
To make an egg do what it don't want to do
Strikes me like a difficult sort of a task.

ALL OF WHICH is pure nonsense. Of course. Who ever heard of an egg either behaving or misbehaving? Nobody. That is, nobody that I know, unless it be Blacky. It is best not to mention eggs in Blacky's presence these days. They are a forbidden topic when he is about. Blacky is apt to be a little resentful at the mere mention of an egg. I don't know as I wholly blame him. How would you feel if you *knew* you knew all there was to know about a thing, and then found out that you didn't know anything at all? Well, that is the way it is with Blacky the Crow.

If any one had told Blacky that he didn't know all there is to know about eggs, he would have laughed at the idea. Wasn't he, Blacky, hatched from an egg himself? And hadn't he, ever since he was big enough, hunted eggs and stolen eggs and eaten eggs? If he didn't know about eggs, who did? That is the way he would have talked before his visit to Farmer Brown's henhouse. It is since then that it has been unwise to mention eggs when Blacky is about.

When Blacky saw the two eggs in the nest in Farmer Brown's henhouse how Blacky did wish that he could take both. But he couldn't. One would be all that he could manage. He must take his choice and go away while the going was good. Which should he take?

It often happens in this life that things which seem to be unimportant, mere trifles in themselves, prove to be just

the opposite. Now, so far as Blacky could see, it didn't
make the least difference which egg he took, excepting
that one was a little bigger than the other. As a matter of
fact, it made all the difference in the world. One was
brown and very good to look at. The other, the larger of
the two, was white and also very good to look at. In fact,
Blacky thought it the better of the two to look at, for it
was very smooth and shiny. So, partly on this account,
and partly because it was the largest, Blacky chose the
white egg. He seized it in his claws and started to fly with
it, but somehow he could not seem to get a good grip on
it. He fluttered to the ground just outside the door, and
there he got a better grip. Just as old Dandycock the
Rooster, with head down and all the feathers on his neck
standing out with anger, came charging at him, Blacky
rose into the air and started over the Old Orchard toward
the Green Forest.

Never had Blacky felt more like cawing at the top of his
lungs. You see, he felt that he had been very smart, and I
suspect that he also felt that he had been very brave. He
would have liked to boast a little. But he didn't. He wisely
held his tongue. It would be time enough to do his boast-
ing after he had reached a place of safety and had eaten
that egg.

He was halfway across the Old Orchard when he felt
that egg beginning to slip. Now at best it isn't easy to
carry an egg without breaking it. You know how very careful you have to be. Just imagine how Blacky felt when that
egg began to slip. Do what he would, he couldn't get a better grip on it. It slipped a wee bit more. Blacky started
down towards the ground. But he wasn't quick enough.
Striped Chipmunk, watching Blacky from the old stone
wall, saw something white drop from Blacky's claws. He
saw Blacky dash after it and clutch at it only to miss it.
Then the white thing struck a branch of an old apple tree,
bounced off and fell to the ground. Blacky followed it.

Striped Chipmunk stole very softly through the grass to
see what Blacky was doing. Blacky was standing close

Striped Chipmunk saw something white drop from Blacky's claws.
Page 76

beside a white thing that looked very much like an egg. He was looking at it with the queerest expression.

Now and then he would reach out and rap it sharply with his bill, and then look as if he didn't know what to make of it. He didn't. That egg wasn't behaving right. It should have broken when it hit the branch of the apple tree. Certainly it should have broken when he struck it that way with his bill. However was he to eat that egg, if he couldn't break the shell? Blacky didn't know.

XXXII. What Blacky Did with the Stolen Egg

BLACKY WAS PUZZLED. He didn't know what to make of that egg he had stolen from Farmer Brown's henhouse. It wasn't like any egg he ever had seen or even heard of. It was a beautiful-looking egg, and he had been sure that it would taste as good, quite as good as it looked. Even now he wasn't sure that if he could only taste it, it would be all that he had hoped. But how could he taste it, when he couldn't break that shell? He never had heard of such a shell. He doubted if anybody else ever had, either. He had hammered at it with his stout bill until he was afraid that he would break that, instead of the egg. The more he tried to break into it and couldn't, the hungrier he grew, and the more certain that nothing else in all the world could possibly taste so good.

But the Old Orchard was not the place for him to work on that egg. In the first place, it was too near Farmer Brown's house. This made Blacky uneasy. You see, he had something of a guilty conscience. Not that he felt at all a sense of having done wrong. To his way of thinking, if he were smart enough to get that egg, he had just as much right to it as any one else, particularly Farmer Brown's boy. Yet he wasn't at all sure that Farmer Brown's boy would look at the matter quite that way. In fact, he had a feeling that Farmer Brown's boy would call him a thief if he should be discovered with that egg. Then, too, there were too many sharp eyes in the Old Orchard. He wanted to get away where he could be sure of being alone. Then if he couldn't break that shell, no one would be the wiser. So he picked up the egg and flew straight over to the

Green Forest, and this time he managed to get there without dropping it.

Now you would never suspect Blacky the Crow, he of
the sharp wits and crafty ways, of being amused by bright
things, would you? But he is. In fact, Blacky is quite like a
little child in this matter. Anything that is bright and shiny
interests Blacky right away. If he finds anything of this
kind, he will take it away to a certain secret place, and
there he will admire it and play with it and finally hide it.
If I didn't know that it isn't so, because it couldn't possibly be so, I should think that Blacky was some relation to
certain small boys I know. Always their pockets are filled
with all sorts of useless odds and ends which they have
picked up here and there. Blacky has no pockets, so he
keeps his treasures of this kind in a secret hiding-place, a
sort of treasure storehouse. He visits this secretly every
day, uncovers his treasures, and gloats over them and
plays with them, then carefully covers them up again.

First Blacky took this egg over near his home, and there
he once more tried and tried and tried to break the shell.
But the shell wouldn't break, not even when Blacky quite
lost his temper and hammered at it for all he was worth.
Then he gave the thing up as a bad matter and flew up to
his favorite roost in the top of a tall pine-tree, leaving the
egg on the ground. But from where he sat on his favorite
roost in the tall pine-tree he could see that provoking egg,
a little spot of shining white. When a Jolly Little Sunbeam
found it and rested on it, it was so very bright and shiny
that Blacky couldn't keep his eyes off it.

Little by little he forgot that it was an egg. At least, he
forgot that he wanted to eat it. He began to find pleasure
in just looking at it. It might not satisfy his stomach, but it
certainly was very satisfying to his eyes. He forgot to
think of it as a thing to eat, but began to think of it wholly
as a thing to look at and admire. He was glad he hadn't
been able to break that shell.

Once more he spread his black wings and flew down to
the egg. He cocked his head to one side and looked at it.

He cocked his head to the other side and looked at it. He walked all around it, chuckling and saying to himself, "Pretty, pretty, pretty, pretty and all mine, mine, mine, mine! Pretty, pretty, and all mine!"

Than he craftily looked all about to make sure that no one was watching him. Having made quite sure, he rolled the egg over and turned it around and admired it to his heart's content. At last he picked it up and carried it to his treasure-house and covered it over very carefully. And there that china nest-egg, for that is what he had stolen, is still his chief treasure to this day, and Blacky still sometimes wonders what kind of a hen laid such a hard-shelled egg.

Blacky has had very many other adventures, but it would take another book to tell about all of them. That would be hardly fair to some of the other little people who also have had adventures and want them told to you. One of these is a beautiful little fellow who lives in the Green Forest, and so the next book will be Whitefoot the Wood Mouse.